DISNEY
FROZEN

ANNA'S ICY ADVENTURE

randomhouse.com/kids

ISBN 978-0-7364-8132-8 (trade)
ISBN 978-0-7364-3115-6 (lib. bdg.)

Printed in the United States of America
10 9 8 7 6 5 4 3 2 1

DISNEP
FROZEN

ANNA'S ICY ADVENTURE

Adapted by Elise Allen

Illustrated by Denise Shimabukuro

Golden® First Chapters
A GOLDEN BOOK • NEW YORK

CHAPTER 1

For as long as I can remember, the kingdom of Arendelle has been shut off from the rest of the world, especially the castle, with its locked gates, closed doors, and shuttered windows. That means the royal family—including me—has been the most closed off of all.

I'm Anna, Princess of Arendelle. It's a fancy title that sounds very regal and proper, but I'm not like that. I'd rather run around with the wind in my hair and experience new things! If only I were allowed off the castle grounds, which I'm not. I used to beg my mother and father to change the rule, but they said it was necessary to keep Elsa and me safe.

I didn't like it, but I trusted them. That's why, after the terrible shipwreck that took our parents away, I didn't complain when the castle stayed as closed off as ever.

Elsa, by the way, is my older sister. She *never* complains about the rule. She says as members of the royal family, we have responsibilities that are far more important than any little things we might want.

That's Elsa. She's a perfectly poised, proper and polished princess. Soon she'll be an equally perfect queen. She's very dedicated to Arendelle, and we're lucky to have her as our future leader.

I just wish she were a little more dedicated to *me*.

Don't get me wrong. She's not mean to me or anything. She just . . . doesn't seem to like me very much. It's weird, because when we were little, we used to play together all the time. We especially loved winter. I remember we'd make snow angels, build snowmen, and have huge snowball fights. We'd laugh so hard we couldn't even breathe!

Then, when I was about five years old, everything changed. Out of nowhere, Elsa stopped liking me.

All of a sudden, every time I knocked on her door, she'd yell at me to go away.

I didn't get it. I *still* don't get it. What did I do to make her so upset? I feel like if I knew, I could make it better. I always *tried* to make it better. I invited her to play with me. I sent her little notes. I asked her what she was thinking about so maybe she'd start talking . . . but nothing I did helped.

The whole thing makes me really sad, but I can't force Elsa to like me if she doesn't. Besides, today my whole world will change. It's Elsa's coronation day. In just a few hours, she'll take the oath and become Queen of Arendelle. By law, everyone is invited to witness the event. All of Arendelle will pour into our castle walls. Finally, I'll have the chance to meet new people and make friends!

I could even fall in love.

I can picture exactly how it will happen. I'll see him across the crowd. He'll be tall and handsome.

Our eyes will meet. I'll give him a secret smile. He'll think I'm sophisticated and fascinating. We'll walk toward each other like there's no one else in the world. Then, from the minute we say hello, we'll know we'll always be together. He'll love me forever, and he won't ever turn on me for no apparent reason, like some people I know.

I throw myself into my closet to find my coronation dress. I toss it on, then spin over to the mirror. I pin up my strawberry-blond hair. A thatch of white runs through it.

Did I mention I have a single streak of white hair? I was born with it, although I dreamed I was kissed by a troll.

Suddenly, I hear loud creaks and groans. It has to be the sound of the castle gates opening! I race into the hall but stop at Elsa's closed door. I wonder if she's nervous. Maybe I should try to talk to her.

There's no point. She'll only tell me to go away. Instead I run downstairs and into the courtyard, which is already filling with guests. I try to smile and look friendly, but when people see me, they won't meet my eyes. They bow and hurry on their way.

I guess it's not so easy for a princess to meet new people.

I'm disappointed, but if I can't make a new friend, maybe I can at least slip outside the castle grounds for a little bit. It's such a gorgeous summer day, and the water surrounding our kingdom glistens in the sunlight. I head to the docks, where beautifully decorated boats stream in from all over. I'm so amazed by their high masts and multicolored flags, I don't even look where I'm going.

That's probably why I'm shocked when a horse slams into me. It sends me toppling backward into a boat, and my weight tips the boat off the dock!

Oh, no! I can be so clumsy.

At the last second, the horse stops the boat with his hoof.

"I'm so sorry. Are you hurt?" a voice asks.

Surely that can't be the horse.

I look up, and there is the most handsome man
I've ever seen in my life.

CHAPTER 2

The man hops down from his horse. He steps into the boat with me and offers his hand.

"Prince Hans of the Southern Isles," he says.

He's a prince? An actual "handsome prince"?

I guess I can forgive him for slamming his horse into me.

"Princess Anna of Arendelle," I say.

Prince Hans drops to his knees and bows his head. His horse bows, too—and takes his hoof off the boat! The boat tips, sending Hans and me sprawling into each other.

It's a little embarrassing.

Hans turns bright red and apologizes stiffly for tackling "the Princess of Arendelle." I realize he thinks I'm the princess who is about to become queen, which would be funny if it weren't so ridiculous. I tell him not to worry. I'm not Elsa, I'm just me.

"Just you?" he asks.

He smiles. He has a really great smile. I want to say something clever, but then the Arendelle chapel bells ring. It's time for the coronation! I wave goodbye to Hans and run as fast as I can to catch the ceremony.

Elsa's coronation is beautiful. I stand right next to her at the front of the chapel. When I peek past the bishop, I can see the entire audience. I can't believe how many people are here! I look for Hans, and he waves when I spot him.

See? I've only spent a few minutes out of the castle and I've already made a friend! I want to tell Elsa, but she's a little busy becoming queen.

I watch the bishop put the crown on Elsa's head. Then he picks up a pillow holding the royal scepter and orb. She reaches for them, but the bishop stops her before she touches them.

"Your gloves, Your Majesty," he says.

Elsa always wears gloves, even when it's hot out. I don't know why. I've asked her, but she never answers. I guess she just likes them, which makes sense. The gloves are beautiful on her, but the ritual requires her to take the scepter and orb with bare hands.

It shouldn't be a big deal for Elsa to take off the gloves, but she looks really nervous. I understand. It's a huge responsibility to become queen. I want to tell her it's okay and I'm here for her, but I don't get the chance. She takes a deep breath, pulls off her gloves, and hands them to me, then picks up the orb and scepter.

Elsa turns around to face the crowd. She holds the orb and scepter high as the bishop proclaims her Queen of Arendelle.

I hear everyone cheer, but I can't stop staring at Elsa. She looks pale. I wonder if she's okay.

A second later, it's over. Elsa puts down the

orb and scepter, whips her gloves out of my hands, and quickly puts them back on. The whole crowd applauds, and Elsa finally looks relaxed. She even smiles at me!

Later, we stand together as trumpets announce our arrival at the coronation ball in the Great Hall.

"Ladies and gentlemen, Queen Elsa and Princess Anna!" the heralds call.

We walk in together, and I gasp. The room is magnificent! It's filled with dancers, all of whom turn to applaud as we enter. Tables have been laid with incredible food, and the walls are draped in beautiful decorations. I'm so amazed that I giggle, and I'm afraid Elsa will scold me for being inappropriate. Instead she squeezes my hand and smiles—again!

We're ushered to the head of a receiving line, where an endless row of dignitaries wait to shake our hands. The Duke of Weselton is first in line and asks Elsa to dance. She replies, "I do not dance. But my sister does."

For a second I think Elsa wants to get rid of me, but then I see the gleam in her eye. She's trying to hold in a laugh, and as the Duke whisks me onto the floor I realize why. The man dances like a sprightly peacock, mincing and preening with no clue that he's stepping all over my feet!

When he finally returns me to Elsa's side, I try to glare at her, but the minute our eyes meet we both burst out laughing.

I can't believe it—we're really having fun together! Maybe all this time, Elsa was just worried about becoming queen. Now that it has happened, she can finally relax, and we'll be friends again.

"I wish it could be like this all the time," I say.

"Me too," Elsa replies, and I feel my heart soar. Then her smile fades and she adds, "But that can't be."

Is she serious? Why can't it? I want to ask, but I know the look on her face. She's already shut me out. Whatever we had, it's over.

I excuse myself and walk away. I don't know where I'm going, but I can't stay there next to Elsa. Unfortunately, the party is so packed with people it's impossible to get anywhere. Again and again I'm pulled into the dancing, and I am *not* a good dancer. I get bumped by a conga line, slip on my own dress, and fall . . . right into the arms of Prince Hans!

Unlike me, Hans is a terrific dancer. He whirls me around on the dance floor, and in his arms I'm light on my feet. We dance until we're completely

out of breath. I'm having so much fun, I'm not even thinking about Elsa anymore.

Afterward, Hans and I walk around the castle and talk. I learn all about him. It turns out he has twelve older brothers—*twelve!* I tell him everything. He's such a great listener that it's easy. We make each other laugh, and we have so much in common that soon we're finishing each other's sentences.

Even though we just met, I know it's true love. Hans knows it, too. He's so sure, he asks me to marry him! Of course I say yes.

I can't wait to tell Elsa the great news.

CHAPTER 3

Hans and I find Elsa back in the Great Hall. She's talking to some important-looking people, but we pull her away.

"Elsa, this is Prince Hans of the Southern Isles," I say. "We would like your blessing . . . of our marriage!"

"Anna," Elsa says, "you can't marry a man you just met."

That's sweet. She's concerned about me. Still, she doesn't understand what Hans and I have: true love. I explain that to Elsa.

"What do you know about true love?" she snaps at me.

"More than you," I counter. "All you want is to be alone."

Elsa ignores me. Then she tells the royal handlers to end the party and close the gates. She tries to walk away, but I won't let her. I grab for Elsa—and her glove peels off into my hand.

Elsa spins and lunges at me. "Give me my glove!" she demands.

Of course. She cares way more about her glove than she cares about me. I hold it out of her reach to keep her attention.

"No," I say. "Listen to me. I can't live like this anymore."

"Then leave," she says.

The words hit me like a punch.

"What did I ever do to you?" I ask. "Why do you shut me out? Why do you shut the world out? What are you so afraid of?"

"Enough!" Elsa shouts . . . and *ice* seems to shoot from her hand! It spirals across the floor, freezing it solid. Party guests teeter, barely catching themselves on the newly slippery surface.

Everyone is silent for what seems like forever.

"Sorcery," a duke says. As the word echoes through the room, the whole crowd turns and stares at Elsa. She looks trapped and confused. She races out of the hall.

A second ago I was mad at her, but I'm not anymore. I'm worried. I push past everyone to get outside. When I do, I can't believe what I see.

Ice is everywhere. The fountain, the staircase in front of the castle—it's all covered in ice. Finally, I see Elsa. She's at the fjord's edge, backing away from the townspeople. They look terrified, but so does Elsa. I beg her to stop and come back, but instead she puts a foot on the water. It freezes solid.

As Elsa runs away, the water keeps freezing under her feet. I try to follow, but I slip and fall. By the time I look up, Elsa has run impossibly far. She's all the way across the fjord, scrambling up a mountain on the other side. The fjord itself is completely frozen. Every boat in the water is

locked in ice. I stare after her, letting it all sink in.

Elsa has the ability to turn things to ice!

Has she always had that power? Is *that* why she wears gloves?

Helplessly, I watch Elsa disappear over the mountain. My heart aches for her. It must have been so hard to keep her power a secret all these years. No wonder she was always so cold and distant. If anyone got close, they might have found out.

Even me.

My heart thuds in my chest as I realize it. *That's*

why she always shut me out! It wasn't that she hated me, it was that she was afraid I'd discover her secret!

If only she'd trusted me. I wouldn't have judged her. I'd have helped! She could have relied on me instead of pushing me away.

Maybe she doesn't know that, but I can prove it to her. I'll find her and show her I'm on her side. It will change everything. She'll know we're in this together, and we'll be close again.

"I'm going after her," I say as it starts to snow. I don't realize Hans is right behind me until he tries to talk me out of it. He says it's too dangerous. He volunteers to go himself, but I won't let him. I need to assure my sister that she's not alone.

Then the duke who accused Elsa of sorcery shouts to the townspeople that they should all go after "the monster."

"No!" I cut him off. "Elsa is not a monster, and this is not her fault. It's my fault. I pushed her. Please trust me. I will bring her back and make this right. I promise." I hope they believe me.

Before I leave, I tell everyone that while I'm gone, all my royal powers belong to Hans, my fiancé. He's surprised, but he promises me and the townspeople that he will keep Arendelle safe until I return.

I'm lucky I met such a great guy. Elsa will see that, too. She was only worried because she cares. Now all I have to do is find her and bring her back, and everything will be perfect.

CHAPTER 4

Wow. When Elsa creates a storm, she doesn't fool around. It's *freezing* up here on this mountain! I huddle on my horse and pull my cloak tighter around me, but the wind slices right through it.

I don't know how long I've been following Elsa, but I can't see Arendelle anymore. I can't see much of anything through the swirling snow. I try to steer my horse up the same path Elsa took, but I have no idea if I'm going the right way.

A branch snaps and startles my horse. I comfort him, but then we hear wolves howl in the distance. My horse rears up, and I try to hold on but can't. I fly off his back and land facedown in the snow. By the time I sit up, my horse has disappeared.

This is not good. Maybe I should make my way

back to Arendelle. I seriously consider it.

No. My sister needs me. Yes, I'm cold. Yes, I'm lost. Yes, there's maybe a one-in-a-zillion chance that I'll find her in this storm. Still, I have to try.

I trudge up a hill to get a better look at my surroundings. I really should have changed into boots when I grabbed my cloak. As it is, wet snow seeps into my shoes with every step. At least, I think it does. I can't actually feel my feet.

Finally, I get to the top of the hill and scan the area for any sign of Elsa. I don't see her, but I do see chimney smoke from a cabin in the distance. That means a fire—and warmth!

I start to run down the hill, but did I mention I can't feel my feet? They slip out from under me. I tumble head over heels, down, down, down until I splash into a stream. The icy water soaks through my clothes and bites into my skin.

Why couldn't Elsa have had *warm* magical powers?

At least I landed near the cabin. The sign outside says WANDERING OAKEN'S TRADING POST AND SAUNA.

A sauna sounds *amazing*. Maybe I'll bring Elsa back here after I find her. Right now I need winter clothes to protect me from the cold.

I get lucky. Even though the store is filled with summer gear, Oaken has a clearance rack with winter boots and dresses that are my size. While I sift through them, I ask Oaken if he's seen Elsa, but he says I'm the only one crazy enough to be out in this storm.

Apparently he's wrong, because just then a man walks in. He doesn't say hello to me or Oaken. I mean, I know we're all strangers, but we're also caught together in a wild snowstorm. Is it that hard to be friendly?

Oaken tries some small talk. "Got caught in a real howler, didn't you? Wherever could it be coming from? Do you know?"

"The North Mountain," the not-so-chatty guy mutters.

Could be he right? Is Elsa on the North Mountain?

I watch the guy shop for supplies. He definitely knows what he needs for the weather. He grabs ropes, furs, blankets, a hatchet, and carrots.

Carrots?

Okay, so he likes vegetables.

Wait. I could use this guy's help. I mean, I'm pretty adventurous for someone who has almost never left her castle. But there's a slim chance I'm a little out of my league when it comes to navigating magical snowstorms.

"So, the North Mountain, huh?" I say to him as casually as I can. "I'm heading there myself."

"You wouldn't survive," he replies. He pushes past me and takes his things to the counter, but he makes a huge mistake. He fights Oaken on the price. Then, when he's not given a discount, he calls Oaken a crook.

Oaken doesn't take kindly to that. He throws the guy out without letting him buy a thing.

It's a bummer for the guy, but an opportunity for me.

Fifteen minutes later, I'm dressed in a cozy new outfit, and my arms are full of supplies.

Now, where did that guy go?

Soon I hear voices and the sound of a lute playing. I follow the music to an old barn. I peek inside and see my fellow shopper. He's lying against a bale of hay and talking to his reindeer.

That's odd.

No, wait—he is *singing* to his reindeer.

That's even odder.

I listen and realize it's sort of a duet. The guy is singing one part in his own voice and the other part in a fake low grumble, pretending to be the reindeer. It's pretty funny, actually, and as the song goes on I learn a couple of things. First, the guy's name is Kristoff, and his reindeer is Sven. Second, in spite of his man-of-few-words act in the store, Kristoff is a goofball.

That gives me the courage to go ahead with my plan. I burst into the barn.

"I am Princess Anna of Arendelle," I say in my sternest voice. "Take me up the North Mountain. Please."

"I don't take people places," Kristoff says.

He tries to turn away from me, but I throw him the bag of supplies. It's full of everything he wanted to buy at Oaken's, and it lands on his chest with a

thud that sounds painful. Oops. I didn't mean to hurt him.

"Oh, no!" I gasp. "I'm sorry, I'm so—"

When I realize he's smiling. I clear my throat and go back to my stern voice.

"We leave now. Right now," I order.

CHAPTER 5

"So tell me," Kristoff says as Sven pulls us up the mountain in their sled, "what made the queen go all ice crazy?"

I hate to talk about Elsa behind her back, but since Kristoff is helping me, I feel I owe him answers. "All I did was get engaged," I explain, "but she freaked out because I only just met him, you know, today. And she said—"

"Wait." Kristoff cuts me off. "You got engaged to someone you just met today?"

There's a judgy tone in his voice that I don't like. I try to get back to Elsa and her power, but Kristoff's totally stuck on the Hans thing. Obviously, he knows nothing about true love. Yet when I start to tell him so, he clamps his hand over my mouth. I want to snap at him, but I realize he looks nervous. Then he holds up his lantern and I see eyes in the woods all around us.

Wolves.

"Sven, go! Go!" Kristoff shouts.

The sled jerks forward as Sven bolts at full speed. The wolves catch up and surround us.

Kristoff grabs a torch from the back of the sled and lights it as a wolf leaps toward him. He kicks the wolf away, but another one jumps up from the

other side. Kristoff doesn't see it, so I use his lute to knock the wolf away. I save Kristoff, but only for a second. Another wolf attacks him!

As Kristoff is pulled off the sled, he drops the torch and I catch it. The wolf is on Kristoff's back now, and the two of them are dragged behind the sled, Kristoff holding on to the reins for dear life.

I get an idea. I use the torch to light the sled blanket on fire. "Duck!" I yell to Kristoff, then throw the flaming blanket at him. Thankfully he listens, so the blanket lands on the wolf, which tumbles away. I help Kristoff back onto the sled, and we both breathe a huge sigh of relief . . .

. . . until Sven whinnies. There's a massive gorge up ahead!

The next thing I know, Kristoff grabs me and hurls me onto Sven's back. He then unhooks Sven from the sled. Sven and I leap over the gorge, barely landing on the other side, but Kristoff is still on the sled! He clutches his rucksack, gives a mighty scream, and jumps alongside the sled.

The sled doesn't make it. It falls into the gorge and bursts into flames.

Kristoff is luckier. He catches the far end of the gorge, but he doesn't have a good grip. He'll fall if I don't act fast. I tie one end of our rope around Sven and the other end to an axe. With all my might, I heave the axe into the ice, just inches from Kristoff's head. Oops.

"Grab on!" I shout.

He does, and Sven heaves forward, pulling Kristoff to safety.

I look down at the fireball that used to be Kristoff's sled. I feel horrible. I dragged Kristoff and Sven into helping me find Elsa. Now they've lost nearly everything they own, and Kristoff almost died.

"I'll replace your sled and everything in it," I say. "And I'll understand if you don't want to help me anymore."

I walk off. I hold my head high and try to look like I know what I'm doing.

Which way should I go? I take a few steps to my right, but it doesn't seem correct. Maybe to the left? Hmmm.

"Wait up," Kristoff says. "We're coming."

"You are?"

I'm elated, but I try not to show it. I don't want Kristoff to think I can't handle this on my own, which I totally can. Still, it's nice to have company, especially now that it's clear we can count on each other in an emergency.

"Sure," I say as he and Sven catch up to me. "I'll let you tag along."

CHAPTER 6

I don't know how long we walk, but it feels like ages. By morning we've climbed so high up the North Mountain that we're above the clouds. The view is incredible. It's not stormy up here. It's white and crisp and clean and *gorgeous*. Even Kristoff gasps, and he isn't impressed by much.

We walk under a weeping willow. All of its leaves are coated in ice, and they glisten in the sun, tinkling like wind chimes when Sven's antlers brush against them.

"Wow," I say. "I never knew winter could be so beautiful."

"Yeah," a voice replies, "but it's so white. Does it hurt your eyes? Mine are killing me."

Okay, that's weird. I didn't say that. Kristoff

didn't say that. He and I share a glance, then look at Sven. Was it him?

Nope. Sven looks as confused as we are.

"Am I right?" the voice asks again. Now it's behind us. I spin around.

I almost don't want to say what I see, because it's impossible. It's a snowman, but he's *alive*!

"Hi!" he says cheerfully.

I do what anyone would do in that situation.

I kick it in the face.

The snowman's head goes flying toward Kristoff, but it keeps talking! Kristoff is as freaked out as I am. He tosses the head back to me, but I don't want it.

Then things get weirder.

I recognize the snowman.

At least, I almost recognize him. I place his head properly on his body, then grab one of Sven's carrots and press it into the snowman's face.

"I'm Olaf," the snowman says. "I like warm hugs."

Olaf. Yes, his name is Olaf. I know that because I remember a snowman just like him, a snowman Elsa and I made when we were kids. Only back then, he was a regular snowman.

"Olaf," I say, "did Elsa build you?"

"Yeah," he replies. "Why?"

"Do you know where she is?"

"Yeah," he replies. "Why?"

I can't believe our luck! Kristoff tells him that once we find Elsa, we can get her to bring back summer.

"Summer?" Olaf asks. "Oh, I've always loved the idea of summer!"

Kristoff and I look at each other. Clearly Olaf doesn't know that snow melts in the summer. He seems so happy, I can't tell him.

We set out, with Olaf leading the way. Eventually he brings us to a wide expanse of winter whiteness. Jagged crags of ice jut out in every direction, and we have to slide carefully between them to avoid getting impaled. It's almost impossible. Just when we think we've made it, we reach a dead end. A sheer wall of ice rises higher than we can even see. I try to climb it, but there aren't any handholds or footholds. There's no way up.

"I don't know if this is going to solve the problem," Olaf says, poking his head around a corner, "but I found a staircase that leads exactly where you want it to go."

Okay, maybe there's *one* way up.

Sven can't handle the steps. They're made of crystalline ice. He waits below as Kristoff and I follow Olaf. We soon arrive at an ice palace with

spires that reach to the sky. It's stunning. Part of me can't believe Elsa built this herself, but another part feels that it's perfect for her. The palace is flawless and strong . . . and cold.

All of a sudden, I'm worried. What if Elsa doesn't want me to find her? What if she'd rather be alone?

No. That's ridiculous. That's just me being nervous. Elsa's my sister. Now that I know her secret, it's a whole new beginning for us.

I reach out and knock on the door. It swings open. I figure that has to be a good sign. Elsa never opened her door for me before.

I take a deep breath and prepare to see my sister.

CHAPTER 7

Kristoff and Olaf start to follow me into the palace, but I tell them it would be better if I went in alone. I enter an empty room.

"Elsa?" I call. "It's me. Anna."

I slip on the floor and land pretty hard on my rear. I hear her before I see her.

"Watch your step," she says.

She emerges from the shadows, and I gasp. Elsa has always been beautiful, but now her hair is down in a loose braid and her eyes sparkle. She's dazzling.

"Wow, you look different. It's a good different. I mean, not that you looked bad before."

Elsa laughs. "I feel different."

"I'm so sorry, Elsa," I say. I never should have pushed her like I did back at the coronation. She tells me she's okay. She says she's never been better. She even wants to thank me!

"Are you still engaged?" she asks.

I nod and she tells me that if it's really true love, I should marry Hans. She's not going to stand in my way now.

Whoa. "You mean that?" I ask. But Elsa doesn't seem to hear me.

Olaf has come running in the front door.

"What is that?" she asks.

"I'm Olaf, and I like warm hugs," he says. "You built me."

"And you're alive?" Elsa asks.

"I think so," he says.

She kneels to examine him. When I ask her if she remembers us building him when we were kids, she says yes, and I relax. "That's one of my favorite memories," I say.

"Because you only remember the fun, not the magic," she replies.

What?

"That night I struck you with my powers. I could have killed you," says Elsa.

"No, you—" I start, but she doesn't let me finish.

"How do you think you got that white streak in your hair?" Elsa turns to walk away. "I think you should go."

"Go? Elsa, no. Please don't shut me out again. I finally understand. Come back home," I beg her. "You can be yourself, and I'll be right there beside you. You don't have to live in fear."

Elsa gives a sad smile. "That would be nice, but it can't happen. I might be alone here, but I'm free, and I can't hurt anyone. I can't hurt you. Just stay away, and you'll be safe."

"Actually," I say, "that's not quite true. Arendelle is still frozen over, and we'll all freeze to death if you don't bring back summer. But it's okay, you can just unfreeze it."

Elsa shakes her head. Out the palace window,

she can see the storm clouds sitting over Arendelle. Her expression changes. She looks frightened and upset. "I don't know how," she admits.

I try to convince her that everything will be fine. I tell her we'll work together to reverse the storm. If she'll just let me help, I'm positive we can fix everything. We can face this thing together!

"I *can't!*" she finally shouts, and her power bursts out of her body. There's a second when I see the shock on her face, and then I know the ice burst was out of her control.

It hits me square in the chest.

It knocks the wind out of me, but I won't show it. I can't let Elsa know how much it hurts.

"I'm okay. I'm fine," I lie as Kristoff runs in. He tries to lead me out. "I'm not leaving without her," I tell him.

Elsa sighs sadly. "Yes, you are."

She waves her arms and snow swirls together to form a creature. It's a snowman, but not a friendly one like Olaf. This snowman is as large as a house. When it roars, the palace walls shake.

The snowman doesn't waste a moment before grabbing Kristoff and me. It drops us in the snow outside Elsa's palace, then goes back in for Olaf. It tosses Olaf out in pieces! That's when I lose my patience. Olaf is still smiling, but I've had enough.

"It's not nice to throw snow people!" I yell. Then I gather a large snowball and hurl it at the beast. It chases us all the way to the edge of a cliff, where we're trapped. The only escape from the monster is a

two-hundred-foot leap straight down. It's terrifying, but it's our only hope. We jump . . . and luckily land in a soft and cushy snowbank.

"So now what?" Kristoff asks after we recover from the fall.

"Oh, what am I going to do?" I ask, starting to panic. "I can't go back to Arendelle with the weather like this. And then there's your ice business—"

"Hey, don't worry about my ice business," Kristoff says. "Worry about your hair."

"What?" I grab my braid and pull it around so I can see it.

It's true. Even as I watch, a long, thick section turns bright white.

"It's because she struck you. Isn't it?" Kristoff asks. He looks worried. The truth is I don't feel great. I try to play it off like it's nothing, though. I spring up and start walking, but my legs buckle a little. Kristoff catches me before I fall.

"You need help," he says. "Don't worry. I know

exactly where to go. You need to see my friends. They'll make everything okay."

I look at Kristoff, then at Sven. As far as I know, the reindeer is the only friend Kristoff has. I'm fairly certain he can't do anything about my hair. Or the strange cold feeling in my body.

I follow Kristoff's lead, but I can't stop thinking about Elsa.

CHAPTER 8

Kristoff, Sven, Olaf, and I have been walking for a while now. Kristoff still won't tell me about his mysterious friends. He just says that it's important we reach them tonight.

Eventually Kristoff stops at a flat area filled with loose stones. Ledges of rock covered with scrubby grass and lichen rise around us. I don't see any homes.

"Well, here we are," Kristoff says. "Meet my friends. They're more like family, actually."

"They're also rocks," I say. Just then, a bunch of rocks roll toward us and pop open.

"Kristoff's home!" one of the rocks cries. I realize that the rock is actually a grandmotherly creature covered in moss. Suddenly, I understand. These are trolls!

"He's brought a girl!" the grandmotherly troll shouts.

"He's brought a girl!" a chorus of trolls repeats. They surround me and pull me over to Kristoff.

"What's going on?" I ask as I fall into his arms.

"Just do whatever they say and you'll be fine," he says.

The grandmotherly troll climbs on top of a few other trolls to get a good look at me. "Bright eyes. Working nose. Strong teeth," she clucks. "She'll do nicely for our Kristoff."

"Wait. He and I aren't. I mean, we're not—" I start to say.

Kristoff tries to explain. "What she means is that's not why I brought her here. We need—"

"We know what you need," says a younger troll.

Then the trolls start dancing and singing about love. Their excitement is uplifting. I can't help but be swept up in the celebration. Kristoff joins in, too. Soon the troll women are decorating my hair. They seem to be getting me ready for something. Maybe they're going to take away my cold feeling? That would be fantastic. Plus, this is kind of fun!

When I'm finally face to face with Kristoff again, he looks different. Could the trolls be right about us? Are these sparks of love I'm feeling? I look around and see we're standing in front of a crowd of trolls.

One troll steps forward. He's dressed like a priest. "Do you, Anna, take Kristoff to be your trollfully wedded—"

"Wait, what?" I ask.

"You're getting married," the troll priest says.

"No, we're not!" Kristoff and I say together.

That's when a very old troll pushes through the crowd. "That's right, they're not," he says.

"Pabbie," Kristoff says warmly.

Pabbie nods and smiles, then moves toward me.

He's a complete stranger—and a troll—but

there's something so kind and thoughtful about him that I trust him immediately. When he motions for me to take his hands, I do.

"Anna," he says, "your life is in danger. There is ice in your heart, put there by your sister. If not removed, to solid ice will you freeze. Forever."

What? No. That doesn't make sense. It has to be a joke. I turn to Kristoff, expecting him to laugh, but he looks deadly serious.

"So, Pabbie, remove it," he says.

"Only an act of true love can thaw a frozen heart," Pabbie replies.

I don't understand. "An act of true love?" I repeat.

"A true love's kiss, perhaps?" a troll responds. Trolls all around kiss each other, but I shiver. Out of the corner of my eye, I see more of my hair turn white.

"Anna, we've got to get you back to Hans," Kristoff says.

Kristoff helps me onto Sven, then waves goodbye to his family. They seem disappointed to see us go—especially unmarried.

Sven takes off, Olaf holding on to his tail. "Let's go kiss Hans!" shouts Olaf.

CHAPTER 9

Sven runs as fast as he can, but it takes hours to return to Arendelle. I'm not doing well. I'm still cold, but I realize it's a different cold from anything I've ever felt. I'm cold on the inside. It takes all of my strength to stay awake. If Kristoff weren't holding on to me, I think I'd fall off Sven's back.

I'm amazed when we arrive at the kingdom. It was icy and snowing when we left. Now it's completely frozen over and snow blankets everything. I believe Hans's kiss will thaw me, but who will thaw Arendelle?

Olaf peels off in a separate direction. The people of Arendelle are frightened enough. They don't need to see a living snowman.

Kristoff, meanwhile, rides Sven up to the

castle gate, then helps me dismount. Before he can knock, the doors fly open and two of our servants pull me inside.

I want to say goodbye to Kristoff, but I'm too weak. I hear him tell the servants to get me to Hans right away, and to keep me safe. Then the doors slam and he's gone.

It shouldn't matter. I'm about to see my true love. *That's* what I should be thinking about. Instead I wonder if I'll ever see Kristoff again.

The servants lead me to the library, where Hans is waiting. He races to me, and I fall into his arms. He can feel how cold I am, but there's no time to explain.

"Hans, you have to kiss me," I say. "*Now.*"

I try to stand on my tiptoes and meet his lips, but he doesn't let me.

"What happened out there?" he asks.

Okay, I guess there is time to explain.

As quickly as I can, I tell him what Elsa did, and that only an act of true love can save me. I reach for him again, but he still won't kiss me. He scoops me up and carries me to the couch. Then he puts a blanket over me.

The blanket doesn't help. I'm shivering, and it feels like my insides are turning to ice.

Why won't he kiss me?

Hans leans down. Finally, it seems as if he's going to kiss me . . . but then he stops. "Oh, Anna," he says. "If only somebody loved you."

The ice must be getting to my ears, because that

made no sense at all. "What do you mean?" I ask.

"As thirteenth in line in my own kingdom, I didn't stand a chance," he explains. "I knew I'd have to marry into the throne somewhere. As heir, Elsa was preferable, but no one was getting anywhere with her. You, though—you were so desperate for love, you were willing to marry me just like that."

No. No-no-no-no-no. He can't be saying what I think he's saying. He can't.

"I figured after we married, I'd have to stage a little accident for Elsa," he continues, "but then she doomed herself and you were dumb enough to go after her. All that's left now is to kill Elsa, and bring back summer."

Ice fills my veins, but it's because of his words, not just Elsa's blast. I want to scream, but I can hardly move.

This is all my fault. What was I thinking, getting engaged to someone I didn't even know? How could I have been so foolish?

Hans closes the drapes and pours water on the fire, turning the room dark and cold. I don't think I'll make it much longer.

"You won't get away with this," I whisper.

"Oh, I already have," Hans sneers.

I gather my remaining strength and lunge at him, but I only fall off the couch. Hans laughs and leaves the room, locking me inside. I crawl to the door and call for help, but my voice is so soft, I can barely hear it myself.

It's over. I blew it.

At least I know Elsa's stronger than I am. She'll stop Hans, even if I can't.

She has to.

CHAPTER 10

I lie on the floor for what seems like ages, and then I hear something.

It's hard to even move my head, but when I look up, I see the library door handle jiggle.

Is it Hans? Has he decided he can't wait for me to freeze to death, so he'll do the deed himself? Or worse, is he here to tell me that he has killed Elsa?

The door swings open and I brace myself for the worst. Instead I see the face of the snowman I've known since I was little. Is it a delusion?

"Olaf?" I ask.

It's no delusion, but judging by the shock on his face, I look even worse than I feel. He races to the fireplace, strikes a match to light a fire, then helps me move close to it.

"Where's Hans?" he asks. "What happened to your kiss?"

"I was wrong about him," I admit. "It wasn't true love. Please, Olaf, you can't stay here. You'll melt."

He refuses to leave until we have come up with another act of true love, but I shake my head. I say I don't even know what love is anymore.

"I do," Olaf says. "Love is putting someone else's needs before yours, like, you know, how Kristoff brought you back here to Hans and left you forever."

"Kristoff loves me?" I ask.

Olaf smiles. "You really don't know anything about love, do you?"

I notice a small puddle at Olaf's feet. "You're melting," I warn him.

"Some people are worth melting for," he says.

Suddenly, a gust of wind pushes the window open, and freezing air washes into the room. Olaf goes to close the window, but something outside

catches his eye. He breaks off an icicle and uses it as a telescope.

"Huh," he says. "I guess Kristoff doesn't love you enough to leave you behind. Wow, he's really moving fast! Oh, hey—there's your act of true love, right there, riding across the fjords!"

To tell the truth, I'm a little fed up with love at the moment. Still, it's what I need to survive. If Olaf is right, I have to get to Kristoff. Olaf helps me stand. Then I stagger out the door.

I've spent almost every day of my life in the castle, but I don't recognize it anymore. The hallway is frozen solid, and even as we walk, giant blocks of ice burst from nowhere. They push up through the floor like glaciers and block our path. We're trapped.

At least, until I smash through a window and we climb out onto the roof.

The storm outside is worse than ever. The wind is so fierce the snow pelts us sideways. The entire castle is covered in snow. I can hear the crunch and groan of ships trapped in the frozen fjord.

I see Kristoff and Sven reach the castle gate. I have to get to them. I slide down the snow-covered roof and stagger in their direction.

I have so little strength it's almost impossible to push against the wind. My hands feel strange. I look at them and see that they've frosted over.

I don't have a lot of time left. I have to move faster. I have to try.

"Kristoff," I call, but my voice is very quiet. Can he possibly hear me over the howling wind?

"Anna!"

It's Kristoff! He heard me! He sees me! He slides off Sven's back and struggles toward me.

I want to run to him. If he saves me, I can protect Elsa from Hans.

Then something strange happens. The wind stops blowing. Snowflakes hang still in the air. It's as if the storm has frozen solid.

In the sudden silence I hear a sword being drawn.

It's a huge effort, but I slowly turn and see Hans. He raises his sword high above his head and moves closer to a figure huddled on the ground. It's a girl, and her face is buried in her hands.

I gasp when I realize who it is.

Elsa!

I thought she never wanted to come back to Arendelle, but here she is. For a fleeting second I wonder why she came back, but I quickly banish the thought from my mind. With her face turned away, she can't see Hans. She has no idea his sword

is drawn. She doesn't know he wants to kill her!

"Anna!" Kristoff calls.

His voice is so close now, but I can't wait for him to reach me. I summon every last bit of my strength and race to Elsa.

The last thing I remember is lunging between her and Hans.

CHAPTER 11

I feel Elsa's arms around me.

I can hear her crying.

That's weird for a lot of reasons. Elsa doesn't cry, and she never puts her arms around me.

Here's what's weirder, though: I'm pretty sure I died. So how can I feel her hugging me?

Then I realize I can wiggle my fingers!

Warmth surges through my body. I'm thawing out!

The minute my arms loosen up, I wrap them around Elsa and hug her back. She's pretty shocked. She pulls away to look me in the eye. "What? Anna?" she says. "You sacrificed yourself for me?"

"I love you," I say weakly.

Olaf gasps. "An act of true love will thaw a frozen heart," he says.

A smile of understanding spreads across Elsa's face, and I know what she's thinking: if love stopped me from freezing, maybe it will help Arendelle, too!

Elsa raises her hands to the sky, and sure enough, the snow and ice that covers our kingdom drifts back up to the sky. Summer is here again! The sun is warm, and the fjord runs freely. A giant mast rises right next to us. We've been standing on the deck of a boat the whole time.

"I knew you could do it!" I say.

"Hands down, this is the best day of my life," Olaf says as he begins to drip into a puddle, "and quite possibly the last."

"Hang on, little guy," Elsa assures him. She waves a hand and makes a cloud of cold air that sits above the snowman, keeping him perfectly frozen.

Hans, meanwhile, is a few feet away. He gets up and I walk over to him.

"Anna?" he asks. "She froze your heart."

"The only frozen heart around here is yours,"

I say. Then I punch him in the face, and he falls overboard.

That's my way of breaking our engagement.

I see Kristoff smile. I guess I surprised him. He probably had no idea I have a strong right hook. I meet his eyes and smile back.

After the guards take Hans away, Elsa and I gather the citizens of Arendelle and do what our parents probably should have done a long time ago: we tell them about Elsa's gift. She even shows them how it works. She introduces Olaf, then creates a very small snow pile so a bunch of happy kids can make snowmen and snow angels.

Once the townspeople understand how Elsa is unique, they're not afraid anymore. They love their new queen. For the first time since her coronation, they cheer her name. I cheer right along with them, and when Elsa takes my hand and raises it high, I know everything will be different from now on. Better.

As for Kristoff, well, maybe Olaf was right. Maybe

Kristoff does truly love me. I think I truly love him. At least, I think I could truly love him. We only met a couple of days ago. I don't want to think about true love yet.

I *am* excited to pay off my debt. The next day, I lead him blindfolded through Arendelle.

"Here we are!" I announce, whipping off his blindfold.

Kristoff's jaw drops when he sees the brand-new sled. It's the latest model, complete with a cup holder! "Do you like it?" I ask him.

"I love it!" Kristoff says. "I could kiss you!"

Suddenly, he turns red and stammers. "I mean,

I'd like to. I'd . . . May I? I mean, we may . . . I mean, may we? Wait, what?"

I lean in quickly and kiss him. "We may," I say.

He pulls me close and kisses me again.

Did I say I wasn't ready to think about true love? Maybe I'll take that back.

A loud squeal from children snaps me out of my spell. Elsa has opened the castle gates wide. I know what's coming, and I pull Kristoff over so we can join in. Elsa swirls her magic to make an ice rink in the courtyard, and children scramble onto the ice to skate.

"I like the open gates," I say to Elsa.

"We are never closing them again," she says.

And we won't. We're not afraid of anything anymore. Elsa and I know who we really are. Life will be different now.

Except I'll probably always be clumsy. I try to skate, but I'm really bad at it. Thanks to Elsa, I know I'll get a lot of practice. And when I do fall, I know the people who love me will always help me up.